Hiding

To Blair with thanks
for your wit, patience and encouragement.

VIKING
Published by the Penguin Group
Penguin Books USA Inc., 375 Hudson Street, New York, New York 10014, U.S.A.
Penguin Books Ltd, 27 Wrights Lane, London W8 5TZ, England
Penguin Books Australia Ltd, Ringwood, Victoria, Australia
Penguin Books Canada Ltd, 10 Alcorn Avenue, Toronto, Ontario, Canada M4V 3B2
Penguin Books (N.Z.) Ltd, 182–190 Wairau Road, Auckland 10, New Zealand

Penguin Books Ltd, Registered Offices: Harmondsworth, Middlesex, England

First published in Canada by Kids Can Press Ltd., 1993
First published in the United States of America by Viking,
a division of Penguin Books USA Inc., 1994

1   3   5   7   9   10   8   6   4   2

Illustrations copyright © Heather Collins, 1993   All rights reserved
Library of Congress Catalog Card Number: 93-60838   I S B N   0 - 6 7 0 - 8 5 4 1 0 - 7
"Hiding" by Dorothy Aldis reprinted by permission of G.P. Putnam's Sons
from *All Together* by Dorothy Aldis, copyright © 1925, 1926, 1927,
1928, 1934, 1939, 1952; copyright renewed © 1953, 1954, 1955, 1956,
1962 by Dorothy Aldis; copyright renewed © 1980 by Roy E. Porter.
Printed in Hong Kong

HIDING

Dorothy Aldis • Heather Collins

Viking

I'm hiding,

I'm hiding,

And no one knows where;

For all they can see is my

Toes and my hair.

And I just heard my father
Say to my mother-

"But, darling, he must be

Somewhere or other.

"Have you looked in the inkwell?"
And mother said, "Where?"

"In the *inkwell*," said father. But
I was not there.

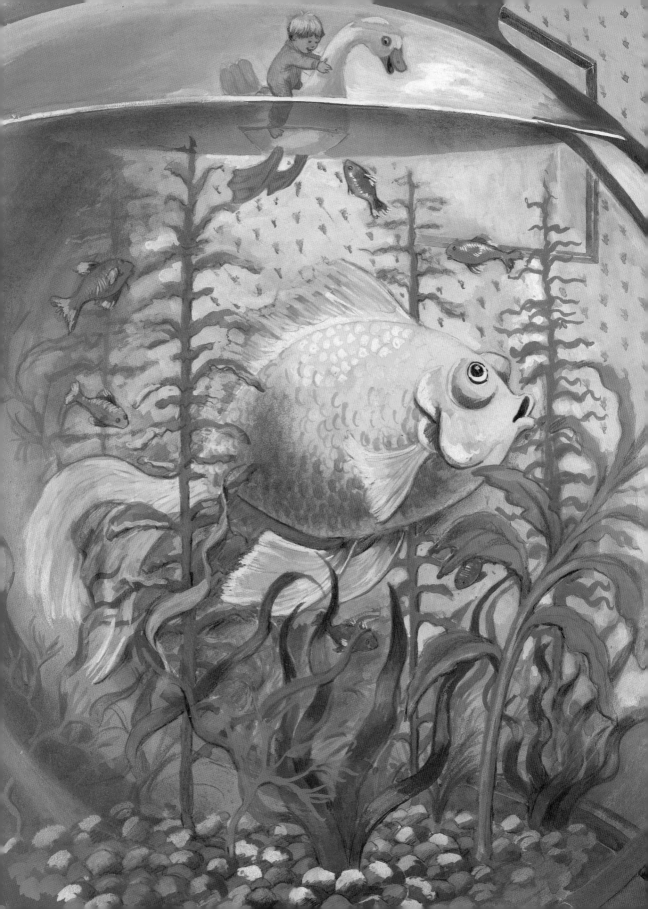

Then "Wait!" cried my mother-
"I think that I see

Him under the carpet." But

It was not me.

"Inside the mirror's
A pretty good place,"

Said father and looked, but saw
Only his face.

"We've hunted," sighed mother,
"As hard as we could

And I *am* so afraid that we've

Lost him for good."

Then I laughed out aloud
And I wiggled my toes
And father said - "Look, dear,
I wonder if those

"Toes could be Benny's.

There are ten of them. See?"

And they *were* so surprised to find
Out it was me!